# MARVEL

# GUARDIANS OF THE GALAXY

## BATTLE OF KNOWHERE

**marvelkids.com**

Little, Brown and Company

Hachette Book Group
237 Park Avenue, New York, NY 10017
Visit our website at lb-kids.com

Little, Brown and Company is a division of Hachette Book Group, Inc.
The Little, Brown name and logo are trademarks of Hachette Book Group, Inc.

The publisher is not responsible for websites (or their content) that are not owned by the publisher.

First Edition: July 2014

Library of Congress Control Number: 2014937170

ISBN 978-0-316-29319-8

10 9 8 7 6 5 4 3 2 1

CW

Printed in the United States of America

MARVEL

# GUARDIANS OF THE GALAXY

## BATTLE OF KNOWHERE

Adapted by Adam Davis
Illustrated by Ron Lim, Drew Geraci, and Lee Duhig
Based on the Screenplay by James Gunn
Story by Nicole Perlman and James Gunn
Produced by Kevin Feige, p.g.a.
Directed by James Gunn

LITTLE, BROWN AND COMPANY
New York  Boston

Peter Quill, Gamora, Drax, Rocket Racoon, and Groot are intergalactic adventurers. Each normally works alone, but they have all agreed to work together. They are on a brief mission to put a very dangerous Orb in a safe place.

As they walk through the streets of Knowhere, Peter suddenly ducks behind a building. He motions for everyone to hide.

"Friend of yours?" Gamora asks, seeing the man Peter is avoiding.

"Not exactly," Peter replies. The man is after the Orb!

Gamora leads the others through a back alley to a café.

Inside the café, Drax looks around, and his eyes light up. There is a small track where little ratlike creatures are racing. Rocket and Groot think this is a great place to hide for a while.

"I am Groot!" Groot says.

As Drax, Rocket, and Groot watch the races, Peter and Gamora listen to music from Peter's home planet, Earth.

Meanwhile, a villain named Ronan the Accuser has been looking for the Orb. He knows it can be used to destroy planets.

Ronan has tracked the Orb to Knowhere, and soon his fleet of Necrocraft arrives in the sky.

Hearing the ships and seeing everyone run for cover, the outlaws prepare to fight.

Peter, Gamora, and Rocket jump into empty mining pods and zoom into the air. Groot moans with sadness. He is too big to fit!

"Wait here. I'll be back!" Rocket cries out to him.

Groot and Drax face down the troops coming out of the Necrocraft ships that are beginning to land.

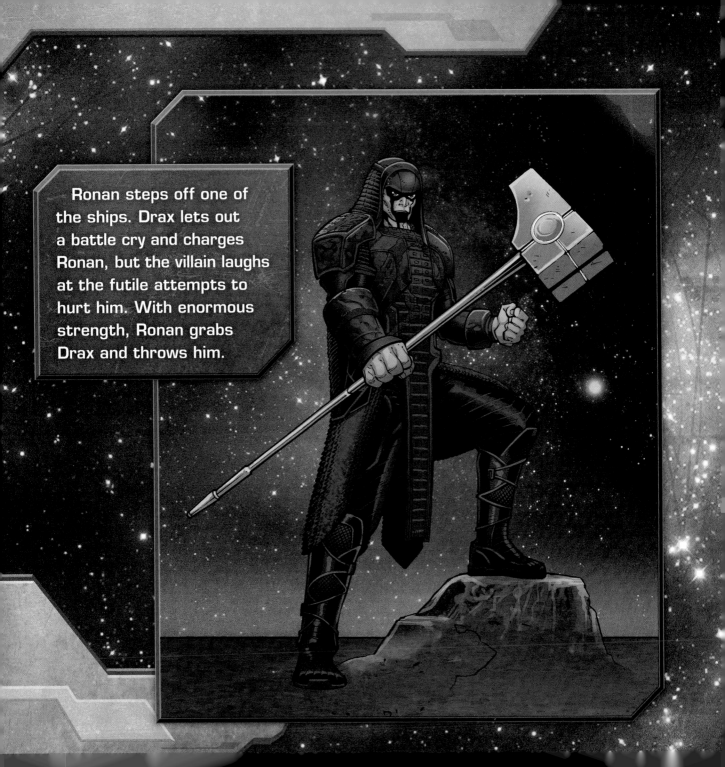

Ronan steps off one of the ships. Drax lets out a battle cry and charges Ronan, but the villain laughs at the futile attempts to hurt him. With enormous strength, Ronan grabs Drax and throws him.

But this only angers Drax more. He gets back on his feet and swings at Ronan with his powerful fists.

While Drax and Ronan are fighting on the ground, several Necrocraft lift off again to chase Peter, Gamora, and Rocket. Ronan's lieutenant, Nebula, commands the squadron to find the Orb. She orders them to target Gamora's pod.

As one of the Necrocraft closes in on Gamora, Rocket slams on the gas and smashes his pod into the enemy craft, sending it spinning out of control.

"That little dude can fly," Peter says to himself with a smile.

Rocket navigates his pod like a pro. One by one, he blasts his way through the enemies.

But his mining pod can't take the hits! His pod is ruined, and Rocket is forced to jump ship. He looks around at all the fallen Necrocraft. He grins and runs back toward Drax and Groot.

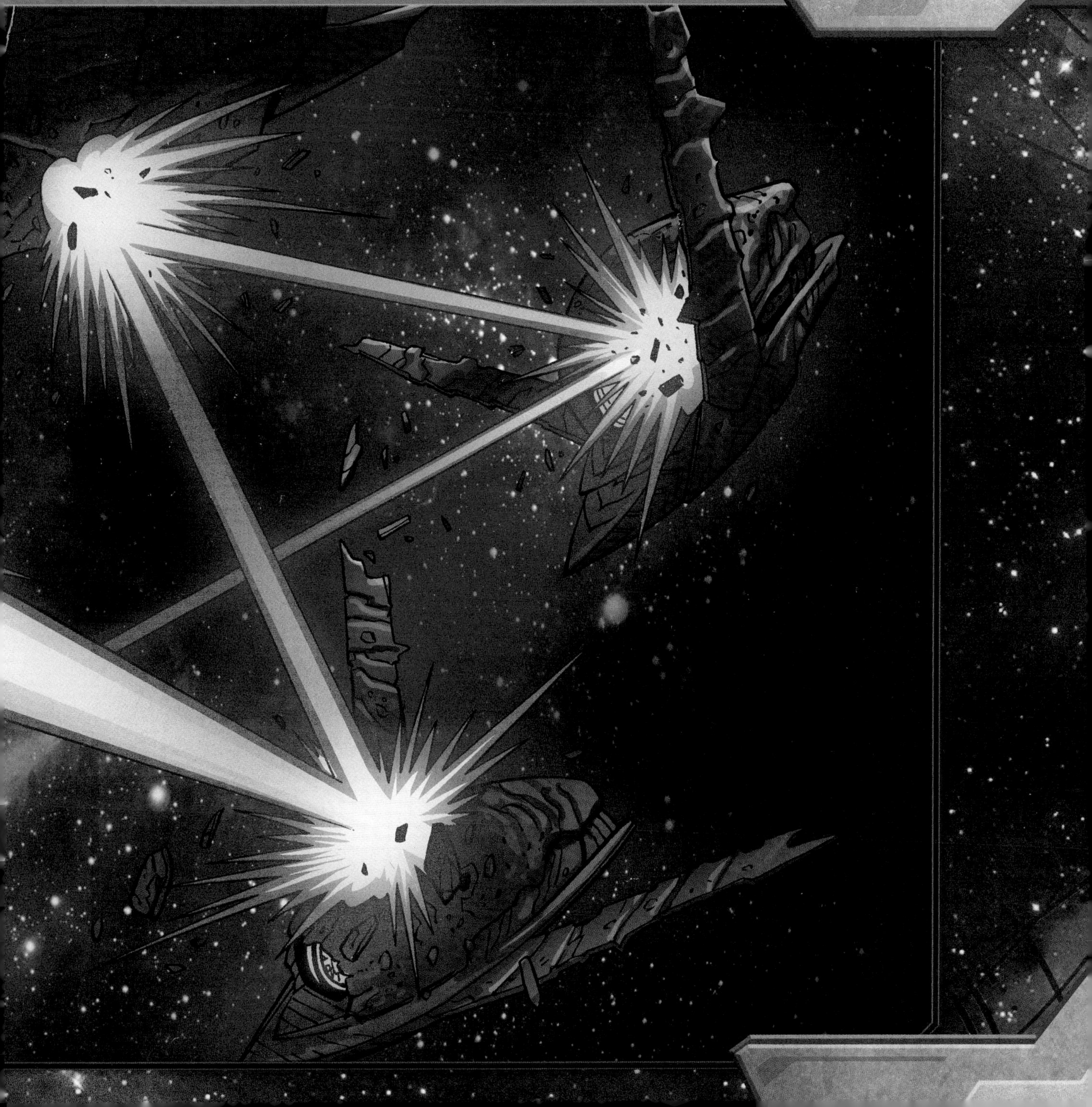

One of the Necrocraft blasts Gamora's pod, and she slows down. Nebula whizzes through the air, coming up right behind her.

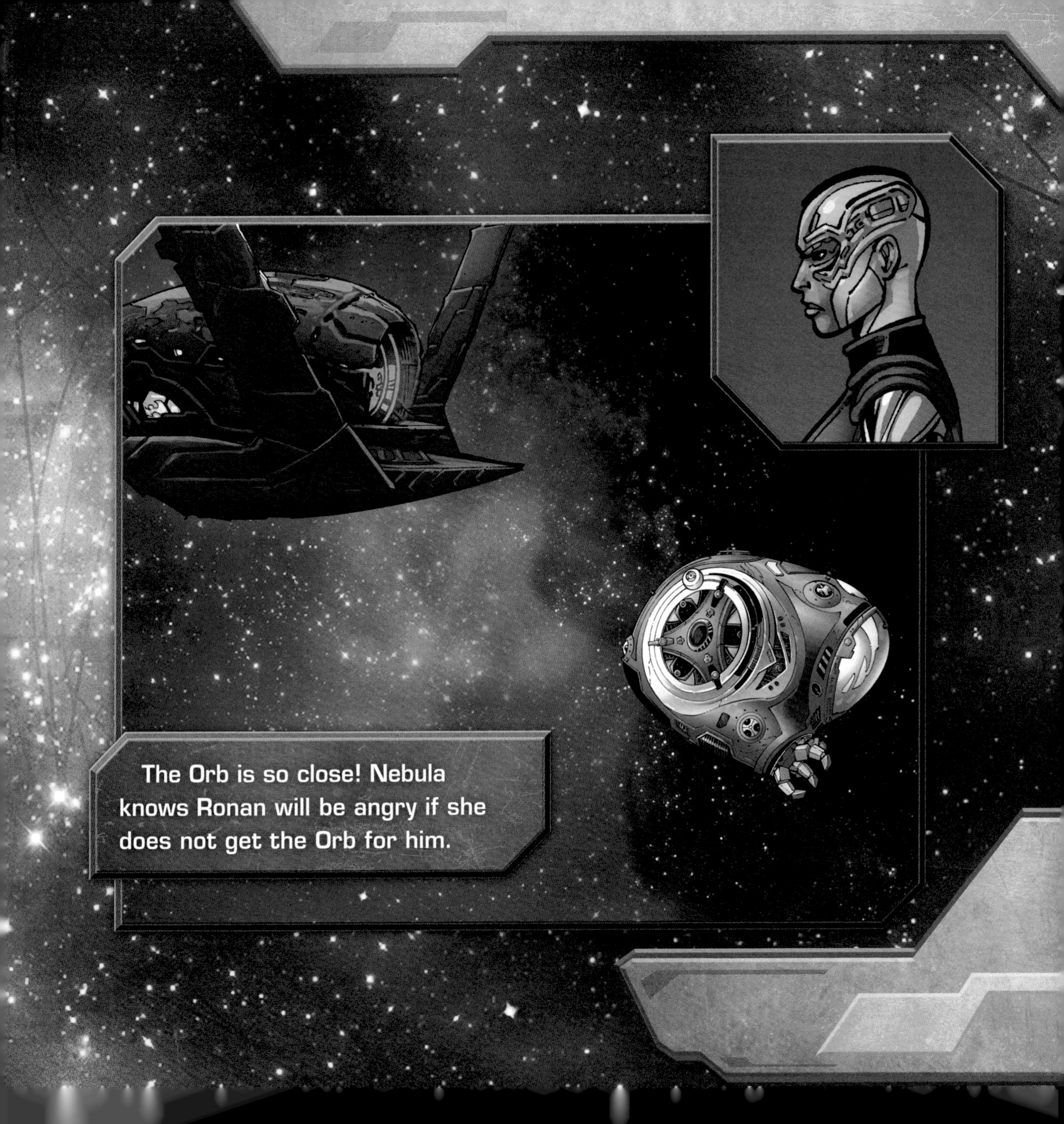
The Orb is so close! Nebula knows Ronan will be angry if she does not get the Orb for him.

With Nebula hot on her tail, Gamora realizes there is only one thing to do. She flies up out of the atmosphere—with Nebula close behind.

"I'm going into the black hole," Gamora says over her pod's radio. "It's the only chance we have!" She knows it's the only way to keep the Orb from the villains.

"Gamora, wait!" Peter yells. Nebula fires a direct shot at Gamora's pod, breaking it apart! Gamora falls out of the sky!

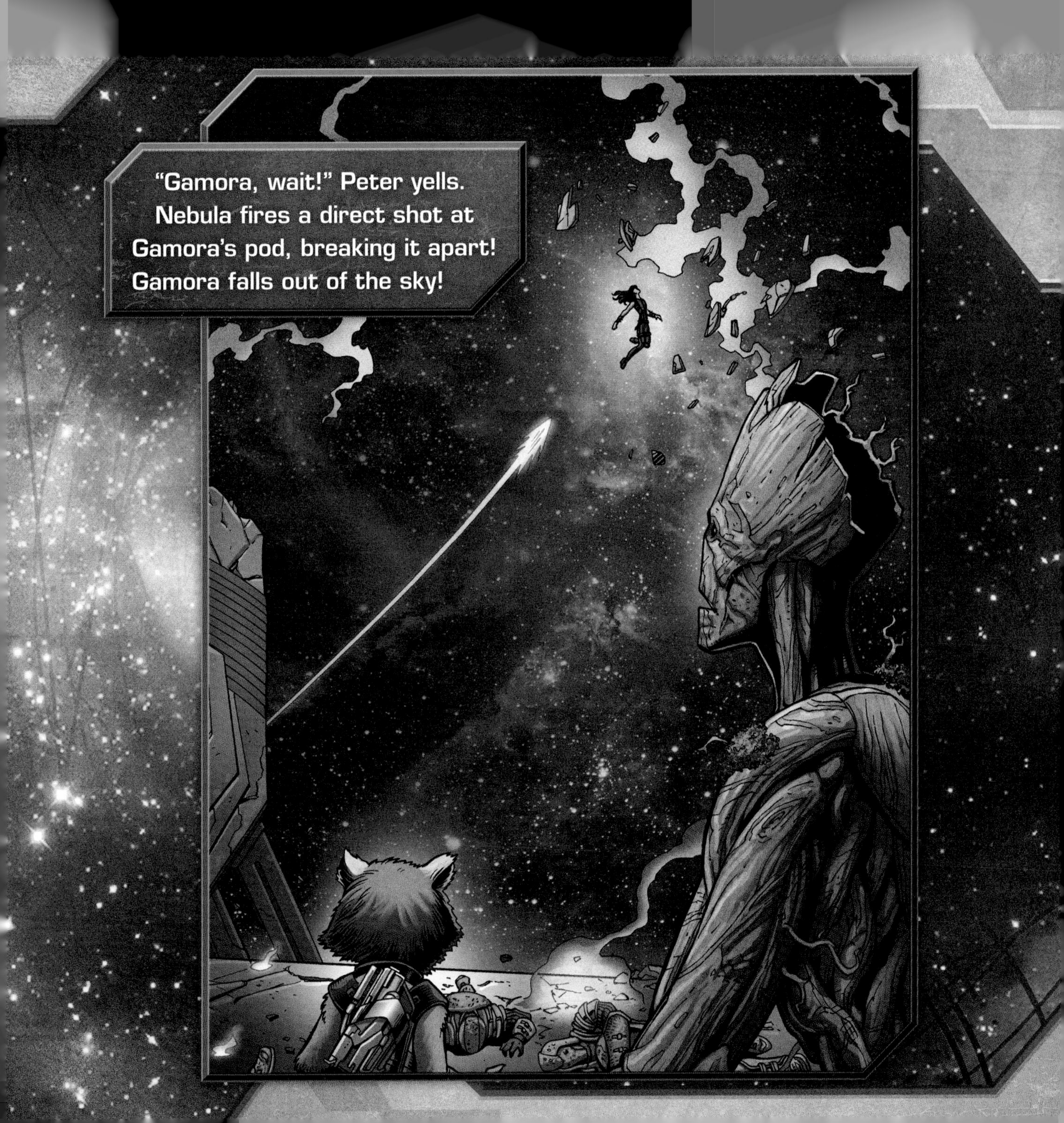

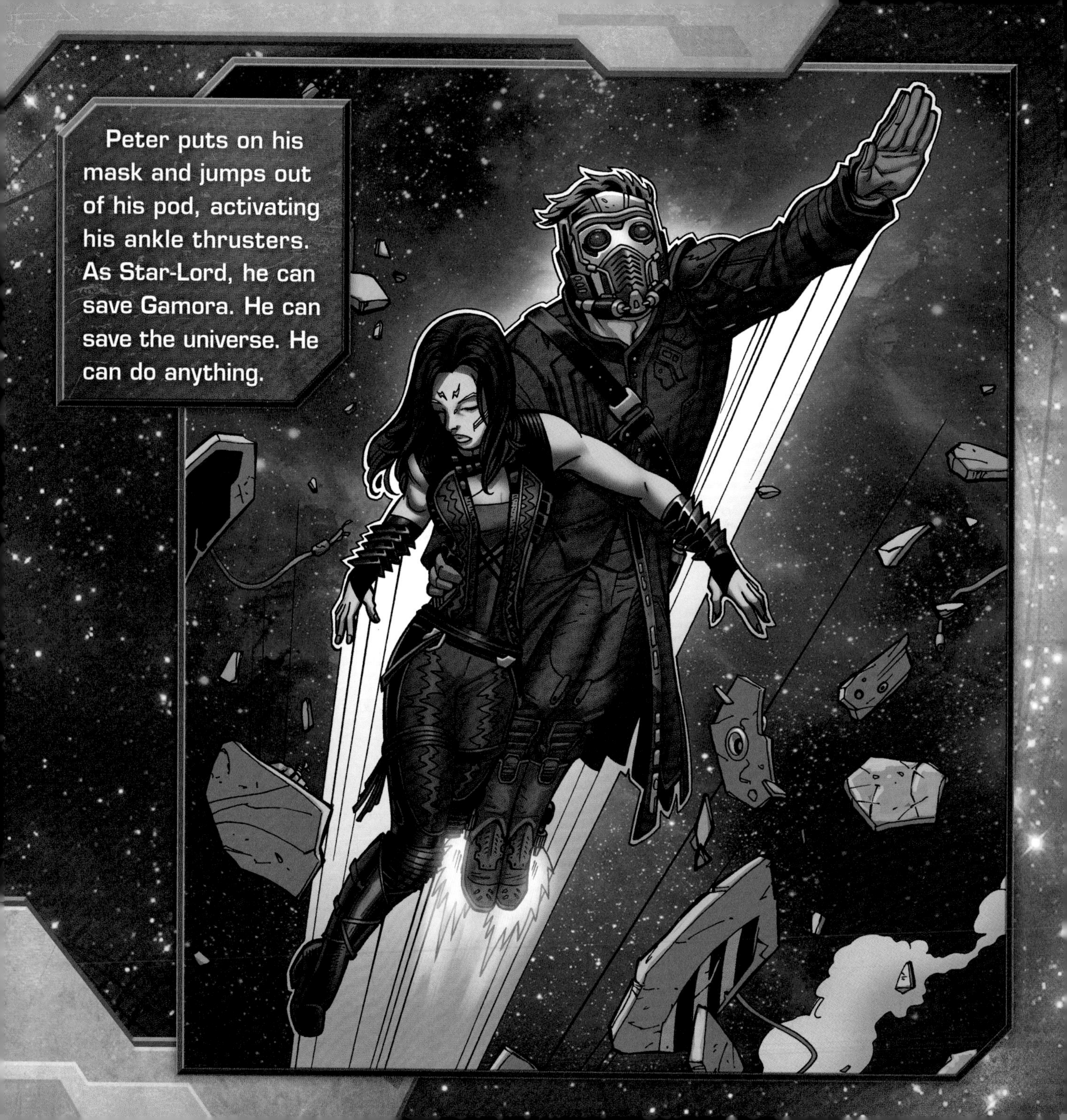

Peter puts on his mask and jumps out of his pod, activating his ankle thrusters. As Star-Lord, he can save Gamora. He can save the universe. He can do anything.

As Peter catches Gamora, Nebula beams the Orb into her ship. She flies away, alerting Ronan that she has what they came for.

Peter lands with Gamora in his arms. She is still alive, and thankful for Peter's help.

Meanwhile, Groot is on the ground battling Ronan's soldiers, trying to keep them off Drax. Rocket reaches his tall friend and helps him defeat the remaining foes.

Getting the call from Nebula that she has the Orb, Ronan flees to the nearest Necrocraft and speeds away.

Together again, the group watches the last of the villains take off after their leader.

"I, for one, can't stand by and watch Ronan destroy the galaxy," Peter says. "We're the only ones who can be the guardians of it."

Peter smiles. The five heroes will now fight together—as the Guardians of the Galaxy!